THIS BLOOMSBURY BOOK

BELONGS TO

....

For Tilly
N.P.

For Arwen
& Jacob
D.C.

Bloomsbury Publishing, London, Berlin, New York and Sydney

First published in Great Britain in January 2011 by Bloomsbury Publishing Plc
36 Soho Square, London, W1D 3QY

A CIP catalogue record of this book is available from the British Library

ISBN 978 1 4088 0000 3

Printed in China by C & C Offset Printing Co Ltd, Shenzhen, Guangdong

3 5 7 9 10 8 6 4 2

FSC
www.fsc.org

MIX
Paper from
responsible sources
FSC® C008047

www.bloomsbury.com

More, More, More!

Dawn Casey

Illustrated by Nick Price

BLOOMSBURY

LONDON BERLIN NEW YORK SYDNEY

'Not krill again!' said Whale.

'Now, now, dear,' said Mum.
'You know they're good for you.'

'Krill are brill,' said Dad. 'I could eat tons.'

'Krill are BORING!' said Whale.
'I want something different.
I want MORE!'

So Whale swam on
till he came upon . . .

Inside Whale . . .

the fish went SPLASH SPLISH.

And Whale went, 'MORE, MORE, MORE!'

So Whale swam on

till he came upon . . .

. . . a slippery, slimy eel.

SLURP!

Inside Whale . . .

the eel went WRIGGLE WIGGLE,

the fish went SPLASH SPLISH.

And Whale went, 'MORE, MORE, MORE!'

So Whale swam on

till he came upon . . .

... a crunchy, crusty crab.

MUNCH!

Inside Whale . . .

the crab went CLICKETY CLACK, CLICKETY CLACK,

the eel went WRIGGLE WIGGLE,

the fish went SPLASH SPLISH.

And Whale went, 'MORE, MORE, MORE!'

So Whale swam on

till he came upon . . .

...a squiggly, squirmy squid.

SQUELCH!

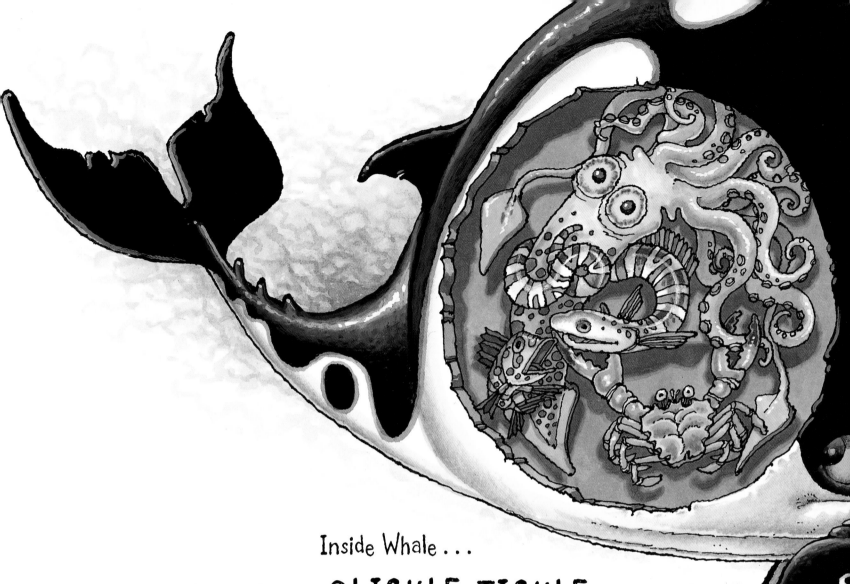

Inside Whale . . .

the squid went SLICKLE TICKLE,

the crab went CLICKETY CLACK, CLICKETY CLACK,

the eel went WRIGGLE WIGGLE,

the fish went SPLASH SPLISH.

And Whale went, 'MORE, MORE, MORE!'

So Whale swam on

till he came upon . . .

. . . a sneery, snarly shark.

SNACK!

Inside Whale . . .

the shark went SNIP SNAP,

the squid went SLICKLE TICKLE,

the crab went CLICKETY CLACK, CLICKETY CLACK,

the eel went WRIGGLE WIGGLE,

the fish went SPLASH SPLISH.

And Whale went, 'MORE, MORE, MORE!'

So Whale swam on
till he came upon . . .

Inside Whale . . .

the ship went CREAK CRACK,

the shark went SNIP SNAP,

the squid went SLICKLE TICKLE,

the crab went CLICKETY CLACK, CLICKETY CLACK,

the eel went WRIGGLE WIGGLE,

the fish went SPLASH SPLISH.

And Whale went, 'MORE, MORE, MORE!'

So Whale swam on
till he came upon . . .

... the whole wide deep blue sea!

SIP!

SLOP!

SLURP!

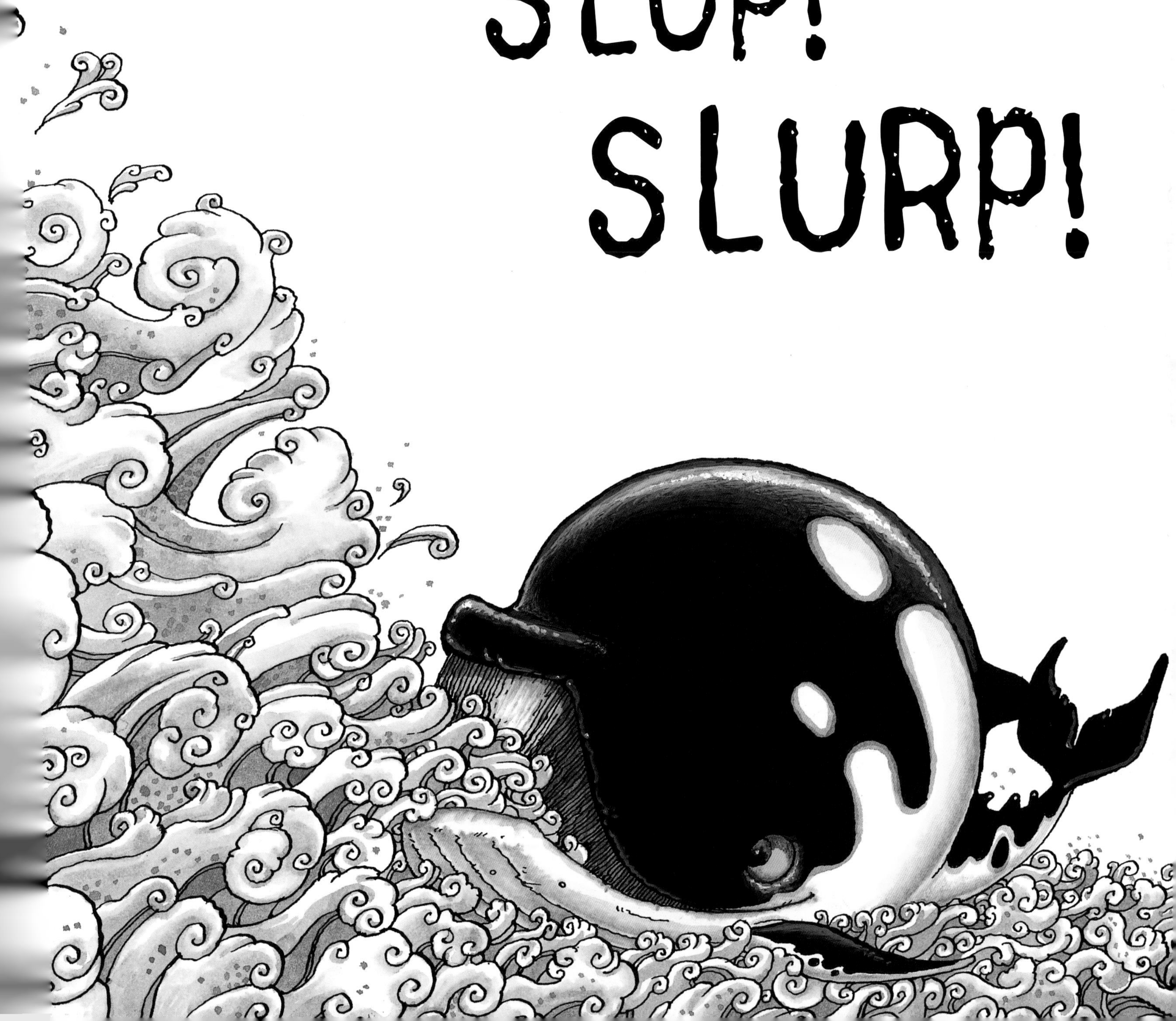

Inside Whale . . .

the sea went SLOSH SPLOSH,

the ship went CREAK CRACK,

the shark went SNIP SNAP,

the squid went SLICKLE TICKLE,

the crab went CLICKETY CLACK, CLICKETY CLACK,

the eel went WRIGGLE WIGGLE,

the fish went SPLASH SPLISH.

And Whale went, '**'OO-ER!**

I FEEL A BIT SICK.'

Inside Whale,
something gurgled and grumbled,
and bubbled and brewed . . .

'What?' said Mum.

'Wow!' said Dad.

'BURP! BURP! BURP!'

went Whale.

Out **surged** the sea,
with a **deafening crash.**

Out **flipped** the ship,
all **mangled** and **mashed.**

Out **shot** the shark,

with a **smirk** and a **swish** . . .

And, last of all,

out **flopped** the teeny, tiny fish.

'That's better!' said Whale.
'But now I'm REALLY hungry.
What's for dinner, Mum?'

'Krill,' said Mum.

'Brill!' said Whale.

Meet more brilliant beasties and curious creatures with Bloomsbury Children's Books . . .

Marvin Wanted MORE!
by Joseph Theobald

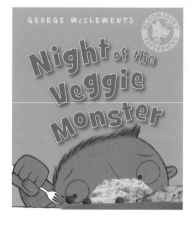

Night of the Veggie Monster
by George McClements

Mr Chicken goes to Paris
by Leigh Hobbs

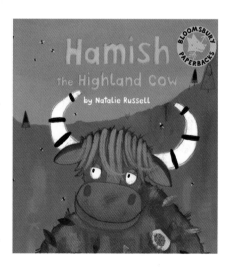

Hamish the Highland Cow
by Natalie Russell